Mariella Mystery Investigates

The Ghostly Guinea Pig

Mariella Mystery

Investigates

The Ghostly Guinea Pig

by Kate Pankhurst

BARRON'S

For the wonderful Claire x

me

TOP detective

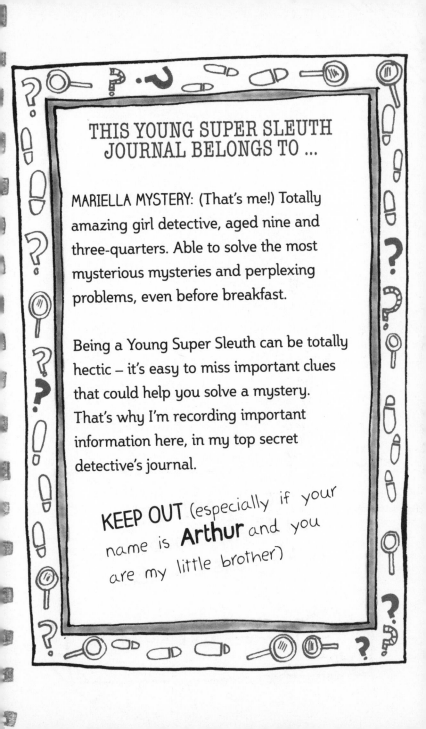

THIS YOUNG SUPER SLEUTH JOURNAL BELONGS TO ...

MARIELLA MYSTERY: (That's me!) Totally amazing girl detective, aged nine and three-quarters. Able to solve the most mysterious mysteries and perplexing problems, even before breakfast.

Being a Young Super Sleuth can be totally hectic — it's easy to miss important clues that could help you solve a mystery. That's why I'm recording important information here, in my top secret detective's journal.

KEEP OUT (especially if your name is **Arthur** and you are my little brother)

MONDAY
April 3rd

cool detective outfit

my house

HQ

8:00 AM
22 SYCAMORE AVENUE (MY HOUSE)

I've only been up for forty-five minutes and I've already solved a mystery. I'm definitely getting better at being a detective.

Here is my case report in full:

7:23 AM: Rehearsals for the talent show are scheduled for 8:40 am in the school playground, so I head down to Mystery Girls Headquarters (tree house Dad built in the backyard) to get my tap shoes. I left them in there after last night's Mystery Girl team meeting.

7:24 AM: I realize security has been breached! The Mystery Girls snack tin has been raided, a pot of felt-tip pens has been tipped over on top of some very important pieces of evidence, and the Mystery Phone handset has been misplaced from its usual position. None of the Mystery Girls would do this. So who could it be?

7:26 AM: My amazing powers of deduction enable me to deduce who the intruder is. Pinned to our notice board, in the section for Mystery Girl team members, is a photograph of a familiar face.

ARTHUR: Aged five and three-quarters, completely annoying most of the time.

empty

SNACK TIN

annoying

11

I have told my little brother, Arthur, he can't join the Mystery Girls because **A:** He is not a girl and **B:** he is too annoying to help me with my very serious work of solving mysteries.

7:32 AM: Arthur (prime suspect) is sitting in the kitchen as if nothing has happened. To make matters worse, he's stroking MY trusty sidekick and cat (Watson).

Watson

I threaten to pour ketchup on his ChocoPops unless he confesses. He denies all knowledge. I know he's lying. Adults are no help whatsoever.

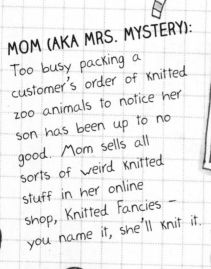

MOM (AKA MRS. MYSTERY):
Too busy packing a customer's order of knitted zoo animals to notice her son has been up to no good. Mom sells all sorts of weird knitted stuff in her online shop, Knitted Fancies — you name it, she'll knit it.

Knitted Fancies

DAD (AKA MR. MYSTERY): Reading the Puddleford Gazette (that's where he works). Successfully ignoring the evidence that Arthur has committed a terrible crime.

7:34 AM: I decide to get a guard dog, or a really fancy alarm system, for Mystery Girls HQ. I'll do that when I've saved up enough money to get the Mystery Phone connected. Mom says having a working phone line in a tree house is extravagant. I say it's essential if I'm ever going to open my own detective agency.

7:45 AM: Case closed, for now.

mystery phone

13

8:30 AM
22 SYCAMORE AVENUE (STILL MY HOUSE)

OK, so that wasn't too hard to solve, but if you want to be a top detective you've got to practice all the time. That's what the Young Super Sleuth's Handbook says. I've been practicing for ages and I feel like I'm ready to solve a really, really complicated and mysterious case now. I've told Poppy and Violet (AKA the Mystery Girls) that we need to keep our eyes and ears open because you never know when a mystery might appear.

essential reading

THE YOUNG SUPER SLEUTH'S HANDBOOK

Being good at solving mysteries runs in our family. Mom always guesses who did it in the whodunit books she reads and Dad has to report on loads of mysterious stuff for the *Puddleford Gazette*. People say things like, "Danger is my middle name." Well, Mystery is my actual last name. Dad says with a name like mine what else could I be but a detective?

me in my DETECTIVE'S hat

SETTING UP A DETECTIVE HEADQUARTERS

Creating your own headquarters gives you a base to solve mysteries from. This could be anywhere – a corner of your bedroom or even a shed. Any space you can make your own is fine, as long as it's a place you can safely store top secret information and you won't be disturbed from vital mystery solving work.

TOP SECRET

Young Super Sleuth Headquarter Essentials:

MYSTERY CORK BOARD:

Display all your evidence, witnesses and suspects in one place to help you solve your mystery.

A MYSTERY HOTLINE for people to contact you on with mysteries to solve.

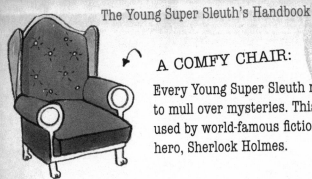

A COMFY CHAIR:

Every Young Super Sleuth needs a place to mull over mysteries. This is the chair used by world-famous fictional detective hero, Sherlock Holmes.

DO NOT DISTURB SIGN (for busy times)

OLD-FASHIONED TYPEWRITER

Stay on top of your case reports.

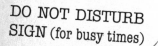

SECURITY SYSTEM

Keep top secret information away from prying eyes.

Young Super Sleuth, Sally McNally (aged 10), created this space-saving under-bed headquarters. It still remains undetected by her parents!

8:55 AM
TALENT SHOW REHEARSAL,
SCHOOL PLAYGROUND

Poppy is taking the Mystery Girls' act for the *Reach for the Stars* talent show VERY seriously. She turned up this morning with a rehearsal schedule for us – every bit of spare time this week is going to be spent practicing our act! Poppy says the other acts have been rehearsing all year so if we want to make a good impression (she means win), we need to stick to the schedule.

complicqted!

POPPY HOLMES: Super cool, super organized fellow Mystery Girl. Very skilled in synchronized swimming. Like me, Poppy has a name only a detective could have. Sherlock Holmes is a really famous detective from a book my mom loves.

POPPY

We thought a trio of tap dancing detectives would be easy to pull off. But today I deduced I have no coordination whatsoever. And Violet deduced she might be better standing still throughout the performance.

"I'm not sure about this, Mariella. What if I end up flat on my face, in front of EVERYONE in Puddleford?" Violet whispered, as Poppy launched into another complicated dance demonstration.

VIOLET MAPLE: Equally cool fellow Mystery Girl. She always knows what to say if you have a problem. Her last name sounds a bit like Marple. Miss Marple also a famous detective from a book.

Violet

(All our last names have something to do with mystery solving. Strong evidence that we are destined to be detectives!)

"Don't worry, Violet. I'll probably fall over too. We can pretend it was part of the act," I said.

We've all been friends since the first day of school and we've been solving mysteries together for ages now (since the Case of the Missing Lunchbox in Third Grade) so I'm sure we can perfect our act by Saturday night. What could possibly go wrong?

11:08 AM
CLASS 5B, LITERACY

Miss Crumble thinks I am finishing off my story.
She won't notice that really I am writing this.
(Journal is concealed inside my literacy book.)
Interesting and possibly mysterious stuff has
JUST happened.

MISS CRUMBLE: Our
class teacher and super
supporter of the Mystery
Girls. She says it's very
important to "let your
imagination run free";
that's why we are
working on a totally great
creative writing project at
the moment.

Miss Crumble

We took turns reading our work. I've been writing this story about a detective dog with the amazing ability to sniff out clues. I got to the real nail-biting part and left everyone on a cliff-hanger (this is a good way to make people want to hear more of your story):

DOUGAL DRAKE, dog detective, dangled helplessly over the enormous vat of bubbling pet food. He knew this could be the end. Would he escape, or would he end up in a tin of his least favorite dog food — Woofles Woofity Wonders?

Usually this was the part where Miss Crumble said how wonderful my work was, so I expected her to at least pretend to be interested. But she was staring out of the window and clearly hadn't heard a word I'd just said.

Eventually Miss Crumble realized I'd finished reading. "What? Oh! Yes, excellent, Mariella! I really enjoyed the part about the dog who, um, what did he do again?"

Unbelievable!

I was suddenly worried that my story might just be incredibly boring. But Dad had said it showed real potential, and it took me ages to write. Maybe Miss Crumble had something else on her mind? Like too much homework to mark or something else teachers do.

It was Poppy's turn to read her story next. Hers was really spooky. It was about a girl who was trapped inside a haunted house:

" ... Brushing a giant cobweb out of the way, her trembling hand reached for the dusty door knob. The bangs got louder, then she heard that sinister moan again, and another terrible bang. She gulped, closed her eyes and opened the door ... "

t-r-e-m-b-l-e

Miss Crumble paid attention to that story. She stared at Poppy with her mouth open.

"Really good, Poppy," she said. "I like the way you described how frightened the girl in the story was. It's upsetting when you can't explain strange goings-on."

Poppy looked at me and shrugged her shoulders.

"Of course, there are definitely no such things as ghosts. Definitely not," Miss Crumble said. Her voice was all strange and squeaky.

Violet turned to me with a dark look that said, Are you thinking the same thing as me?

I grabbed my pencil and, without Miss Crumble noticing (which wasn't hard), I scribbled a note and passed it to Poppy and Violet. It said:

POTENTIAL MYSTERY:
WHAT'S UP WITH MISS CRUMBLE? ??

(URGENT MYSTERY GIRLS MEETING NEEDED AT LUNCH TIME)

Miss Crumble

12:07 PM
LUNCH TIME, SCHOOL CAFETERIA

The Young Super Sleuth's Handbook says that we should be keeping a look-out for strange behavior at all times, and Miss Crumble's behavior was definitely odd.

I showed Poppy and Violet the sketch I'd drawn just before lunch (the Young Super Sleuth's Handbook says observation is a detective's most powerful tool):

Messy hair - no time to brush it

Bags under eyes
Miss Crumble didn't get enough sleep last night

Pale face

mismatched Outfit
MOST unlike
Miss Crumble

Behavior - Twitchy
unable to concentrate
(apart from on ghost stories)

VERDICT: Miss Crumble is showing classic signs of being scared about something

We decided to do a search of the school to find
Miss Crumble and ask if she had any jobs for us
to do. As we set off, I grabbed the Mystery Kit.
Good detectives have one of these on hand at all
times. It's got everything you could ever need to
solve a mystery in it – and my gym kit. (We've
got PE this afternoon.)

the mystery kit

MYSTERY KIT

sweets

binoculars

magnifying glass

camera

gloves

Invisible ink

shorts

evidence bags

P.E PUMPS

There was no sign of Miss Crumble in our classroom, so we knocked on the staffroom door but she wasn't here either. None of the other teachers had seen her all morning. Weird, I thought. Was Miss Crumble avoiding them for some reason?

With only ten minutes of break left, we searched the empty closets and peeked in the teachers' bathrooms.

Nothing.

Then Violet pulled open the door to the art stock room –

Arrrggghhhh!

We found Miss Crumble. "Oh, girls, it's you,"
she gasped. "You made me jump."

Miss Crumble isn't usually the type
to scream because a door opens. She
doesn't normally hang out in closets
at lunch time either. Something was
definitely up.

"We just wondered if you'd like us to do any jobs,"
I said. "And, Miss Crumble, if you don't mind me
asking, why are you sitting in the closet?"

"I just needed some time alone," she said, gazing
into the distance.

Miss Crumble looked as if she'd like us to leave.
But the Mystery Girls don't give up that easily.

"You can talk to us, Miss Crumble. Maybe we can
help?" Violet said. Violet is really good at knowing
what to say in situations like this.

"I'm just being silly," Miss Crumble replied.

"Don't worry, we've heard lots of silly things," Poppy said.

Miss Crumble looked at us and sighed. The Mystery Girl magic was working! She was about to spill the beans.

"Well, maybe you can help," Miss Crumble said. "I'll go crazy if I don't talk to someone about it."

We all leaned in a bit closer. It sounded very mysterious.

"The strangest thing happened last night. I was closing the curtains when I saw something at the back of my yard. Do you remember my pet guinea pig, Mr. Darcy*?"

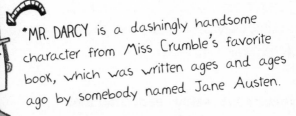

*MR. DARCY is a dashingly handsome character from Miss Crumble's favorite book, which was written ages and ages ago by somebody named Jane Austen.

We nodded. Mr. Darcy was her pet for ten years. It was really sad when he died. I totally understood how she felt because I had a gerbil named Egbert who died of old age. (He was three, which is ancient for a gerbil.)

Egbert

"It was hard to see in the darkness, but it was definitely him. In the shadows, behind my cabbage patch."

"Who, Miss Crumble?" I asked.

Miss Crumble pulled a small photograph of Mr. Darcy nibbling a dandelion out of her pocket.

Mr. Darcy
(the guinea pig)

"I think I saw ... I think I saw the ghost of Mr. Darcy."

No way! We weren't expecting that.

CASE REPORT
MISS CRUMBLE'S SIGHTING OF MR. DARCY
ON SUNDAY NIGHT

**WARNING: THIS REPORT IS VERY SPOOKY.
DO NOT READ IF YOU ARE EASILY SCARED.**

9:30 PM: Miss Crumble decides to have an early night and makes herself a cup of herbal tea before going to bed. She doesn't notice anything strange at this time.

9:37 PM: Before getting into bed, Miss Crumble walks to the window to close the curtains. She notices a small glowing shape at the back of her yard. Unsure what it could be, she puts on her glasses.

9:38 PM: Miss Crumble is in utter shock because there is a ghostly guinea pig, bearing a striking resemblance to recently deceased pet guinea pig, Mr. Darcy, sitting at the back of her yard.

GASP!

33

9:40 PM: Miss Crumble realizes the ghostly guinea pig is sitting on the very spot where she buried Mr Darcy — next to the little statue of him she had made.

(SPoooooKy!)

9:41 PM: Miss Crumble does not believe her eyes, so she closes them. When she opens them again the ghostly guinea pig has vanished.

9:45 PM: Miss Crumble gets into bed but doesn't sleep. She checks her window again a few times but doesn't see anything else strange.

This is a photo of Mr. Darcy when he was alive. He was short-haired with a brown patch on his eye.

Mr. Darcy (alive)

This is an artist's impression of the ghostly guinea pig seen at Miss Crumble's house. It gave off an "eerie green glow." As far as we know guinea pigs don't normally do this.

Mr. Darcy was sighted at the end of the garden, approximately 18 feet from Miss Crumble's bedroom window.

shed

gnome

miss Crumble

SPOOKY!

yoga mat

MR. DARCY!

6:45 PM
MYSTERY GIRLS HQ

I decided to cancel practice for the talent show and called an emergency Mystery Girls' meeting. This case is way too important to waste any time. Poppy eventually agreed and said she would re-work the rehearsal Schedule of Doom (that's what Violet and I have been calling Poppy's crazy schedule) because the Case of the Ghostly Guinea Pig is the most exciting thing ever to have happened to the Mystery Girls.

Violet came up with a really good idea about how to gather more evidence. All it took was an hour's hard work. We are putting our *Have You Seen This Guinea Pig?* posters up around town to try and find other eyewitnesses.

have you seen this guinea pig?

ghostly glow

If you have seen anything strange, get in touch with The Mystery Girls: 22 Sycamore Avenue, Puddleford

"Do you think Miss Crumble really saw a ghostly guinea pig?" Poppy said.

"It's hard to say," I said. "Remember the Case of the Missing Sidekick? When we thought Watson had been cat-napped and he was just asleep in Arthur's sock drawer? There could still be a perfectly reasonable explanation."

"I'm sure you're right," said Violet. "We just need to think about what it could be …"

Logical Explanation 1: Miss Crumble needs an eye test.

Miss Crumble assured us that she can see perfectly well and got new glasses (very stylish ones) only two weeks ago.

Logical Explanation 2: Miss Crumble was tired. What she thought was a ghostly guinea pig was a garden gnome or a pile of leaves.

But Miss Crumble said she definitely saw the guinea pig's nose twitch, just like Mr. Darcy's always used to. That's how she knew it was him.

Logical Explanation 3: There has been a mistake and Mr. Darcy is still alive.

(This could happen, because everyone thought Violet's cousin's hamster had died. Her aunt fainted when it turned out he wasn't dead, just hibernating.)

Miss Crumble said she is very sure Mr. Darcy isn't with us any more. She clearly remembers burying him at the back of the yard.

statue of Mr. Darcy

Poppy is going to put up posters in all the stores around town after school on her way to swimming practice. Violet is going to get her mom to give them out at work, and I'm going to put some up in the bathrooms at school. (If you'd seen a ghostly guinea pig you might hide in the bathroom because you were in shock. If you saw the poster you'd be really relieved to discover the Mystery Girls could help you.)

Dad said he'll put an ad in the *Puddleford Gazette* asking people who have seen a ghostly guinea pig to come forward. He is getting really fed up of having to write news stories about the talent show. He said a ghostly guinea pig  was FAR more exciting than a lady who hopes to win *Reach for the Stars* by making very realistic balloon animals.

If the Mystery Phone worked, it would be ringing off the hook by tomorrow afternoon.

**WEDNESDAY
April 5th**

TOP PRIORITY

SOLVE THE CASE OF THE
GHOSTLY GUINEA PIG

and become world-famous
detective — yeah!

4:30 PM
22 SYCAMORE AVENUE (MY HOUSE)

MAJOR BREAKTHROUGH ALERT!

I was starting to worry no eyewitnesses were going to come forward, but after school today I received new information about the case and raced home.

"What's the rush, Mariella?" said Mom, poking her head around the kitchen door.

"I don't have time to talk, Mom. I need to call Poppy and Violet! I've received new information about the ghostly guinea pig."

"That's fantastic, darling! But now that you're back, could you model this for me?" said Mom, shoving a knitted hat in the shape of a strawberry on my head.

Strawberry hat

It was completely the wrong moment for knitted novelty hats. She's always doing stuff like this. I can't solve mysteries when I'm being distracted.

"MOM! I need to call Poppy and Violet! Roberta Poppet from the Third Grade thinks she saw the ghostly guinea pig on Sunday night too."

"You go ahead and call the girls. I can take pictures of you while you're on the phone. You won't even know I'm here!" Mom beamed.

Arrrrggghhhh!

I bet proper grown-up detectives don't have to put up with this.

I grabbed the handset and dialed Violet's number.

Ring ring, ring ring

"Violet, you won't believe what Roberta Poppet just told me! On Sunday night she went out to feed her pet rabbit, Binky, and she saw the ghostly guinea pig sitting next to the rabbit hutch. She screamed, because it was glowing in the dark, and the guinea pig ran off!"

"Wow. This is huge. That means Miss Crumble did see something in her garden," said Violet. "It means there really could be a ghostly guinea pig on the loose."

"Yes," I said. "And if Roberta's seen it, there might be more people out there who have too!"

Violet went quiet, then she said, "I'm not sure about this, Mariella." (She always says this.) "Do you think we are ready to handle a spooky case? We've never dealt with ghosts before."

"Of course we are!" I said. "We've been preparing for a big mystery like this for ages. We can definitely handle it!"

Mom stopped taking pictures for a moment. "You've just reminded me. I bumped into Hazel Hargreaves at the store this morning ..."

"Mom! I'm discussing a case!" I said.

"It has to do with the case, dear. Hazel said to tell you that she saw a little furry creature running through the bushes."

ghostly

guinea pig

"That's not strange really, Mom, there must be lots of wildlife down there." Mom was reaching Arthur levels of annoyingness – off the scale!

Violet's voice was coming out of the phone receiver now: "Mariella, are you still there? Marriiieeellla?"

"This little furry thing, it was glowing in the dark. She'd never seen anything quite like it," Mom said casually, like this wasn't majorly important information. "Sorry, I should have told you earlier, but I've been so involved with these hats. You look fantastic in these pictures!"

How on earth Mom thought a knitted hat was more important than a ghostly guinea pig sighting, I don't know.

"Violet, did you hear that? There has been another sighting. That makes three!" I said.

Suddenly I heard a bang and the sound of running footsteps on the phone. Had Violet passed out from shock?

Shock!

"Mariella!" I heard Poppy's voice from the phone. She sounded out of breath.

"I just ran here from swimming practice," she gasped. "There's been a sighting! Ben Drummond's dad, the milkman, told me he saw the guinea pig early this morning!"

This was amazing. Now we had FOUR confirmed ghostly guinea pig sightings!

I was about to fill Poppy in on the other witnesses when this totally strange voice drifted out of the phone.

"WooOooooooOOOOOOoooooo.

"What? Poppy, is that you?" I said.

"Wooooo! I'm a ghostly guinea pig!"

"I don't like this. What's going on?" said Violet.

Then I realized. ARTHUR! He was listening in to our conversation on the phone upstairs.

"Get off the phone, Arthur, you GIANT pain!"

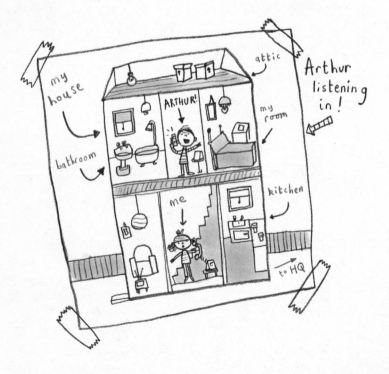

my house

attic

Arthur listening in!

ARTHUR!

my room

bathroom

kitchen

me

to HQ

THURSDAY
April 6th

me →

(Must be kept top secret, I'm trying to be a serious detective.)

HOW TO SKETCH AN ARTIST'S IMPRESSION

It's really helpful to be able to sketch people described to you by witnesses. You won't always have a photograph if the person is a suspect, so creating an "artist's impression" helps you to get an idea of who, or what, you are looking for.

INSTRUCTIONS

1. Ask your witness to give you as many details as they can remember about hair and eye color, skin tone, hairstyle, height, shape of nose, and clothing.

2. Sketch your picture very carefully, making sure you add as many details as possible.

3. Ask your witness to confirm it looks like the person they are describing, to prevent cases of mistaken identity.

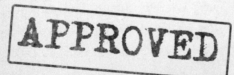

APPROVED

shaggy hair

full lips

If you get stuck with your drawing, try cutting out some of our photo-fit face parts. Photo-fits are used to build a picture of a suspect using pre-drawn sections of faces, like this one.

TOP TIP

Practice your sketching skills by drawing friends and family to make *Have You Seen This Insane Criminal?* posters.

HAVE YOU SEEN THIS INSANE CRIMINAL?

7:23 PM
MYSTERY GIRLS HQ

There is so much to do if we are going to solve
this case. We cancelled our after-school talent
show again so we could interview Roberta, Hazel,
and Ben Drummond's dad (the milkman).

Poppy agreed the case needs to take priority
today but has scheduled in an intensive early-
morning rehearsal for tomorrow. (She said to be
prepared for some serious dancing.)

Even though there are only two days until I have
to tap-dance in front of ALL of Puddleford, it
was worth cancelling our practice session. We've
uncovered something totally shocking ...

Check out these
eyewitness accounts

Eyewitness Accounts

ROBERTA POPPET (AGED 8)

7:30 PM: Roberta goes outside to feed her pet rabbit, Binky.

7:32 PM: Walking back into the house, Roberta hears a shuffling noise. She turns to see a glowing ghostly guinea pig sitting in front of Binky's hutch.

7:33 PM: Roberta screams and the ghostly guinea pig dashes under the garden gate. Binky continues eating his food as if nothing has happened.

The guinea pig Roberta saw was glowing a strange green color and had LONG, messed-up, spiky fur.

LONG! messed up hair

HAZEL HARGREAVES (CHAIRWOMAN OF THE PUDDLEFORD VEGETABLE GROWING LEAGUE)

6:25 PM: Hazel has been weeding her cabbage patch for two hours. It's getting dark so she sets off for home to get tea.

6:30 PM: A rustling noise comes from behind the compost heap. Hazel looks up and sees a small furry GLOWING creature, believed to be a guinea pig, running toward the hedge.

6:32 PM: Hazel investigates but can't see any sign of the mysterious creature.

The creature had short hair and a distinctive DARK SPLOTCH on its bottom. It was giving off an eerie green glow.

splotch

WEIRD

MR. DRUMMOND (MILKMAN AND BEN'S DAD)

5:00 AM: Mr. Drummond travels at full speed down Wellington Street in his milk truck (approximately 5 miles per hour).

5:03 AM: From what seems like out of nowhere, a small glowing guinea pig darts in front of him. Mr. Drummond says that everything happened in slow motion (maybe because his milk truck has a top speed of 5 mph?). He swerves and almost hits a lamp post.

5:04 AM: Mr. Drummond jumps out of his milk truck to get a closer look at the ghostly guinea pig he has just seen, but the street is deserted. Even though Mr. Drummond is still drinking milky tea to get over the shock, he managed to give us this description:

LONG hair ↲

The guinea pig had LONG flowing fur that covered its face and was giving off a ghostly greenish glow.

55

We don't know exactly what's happening but we can say that there are at least FOUR different ghostly guinea pigs on the loose in Puddleford! Long-haired, short-haired, spiky-haired, and spotty ones. (Either that or there is one very strange-looking guinea pig.)

guinea pig Photofit

Flowing hair

messed up

short hair

splotchy markings

8:14 PM
22 SYCAMORE AVENUE (MY BEDROOM)

Violet is worried. She doesn't know how she will feel if she sees a ghostly guinea pig. She thinks it would be totally scary because one could end up haunting you forever. I told her that now is not the time to get spooked out. We need to know more about the ghostly guinea pigs. Like what are they up to? And where did they come from?

outer space?

glowing

Arthur is worried too. After he
interrupted our top-secret
phone conversation
yesterday he refused to
come out of his room.
He kept laughing so I
told him he wasn't safe in his
bedroom. I said we had discovered
that the ghostly guinea pig likes to hide in closets
so it can come out at night and nibble on people's
toes. Ha! He totally fell for it and spent ages tying
his closet doors shut with some of Mom's yarn.
Wait until he finds out there is more than one
ghostly guinea pig!

That'll teach him to be so completely annoying ...

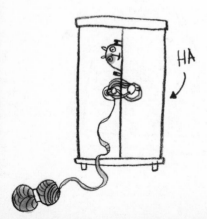

Friday
April 7th

WHERE
are the ghostly
guinea pigs?

BOSSY!

8:30 AM
MYSTERY GIRLS HQ

Poppy was so bossy at this morning's practice session. The talent show is totally stressing her out. (The ghostly guinea pigs are stressing me out, but I am staying calm and collected, like a real detective.)

totally calm and collected and FOCUSED

"If you want to speak, you need to put your hand up," she said, "Let's go again. Wave those magnifying glasses. And step, two, three, four ..."

Poppy's putting-your-hand-up system didn't work very well. Every time I put my hand up to ask a question (which was usually about ghostly guinea pigs), Violet thought I was doing a dance move and copied me. Poppy eventually agreed that we were allowed to talk as long as we danced at the same time.

complicated

HIGH kick

"Do you think we'll need more cookies for our clue-finding mission later? What if we get hungry?" I asked Violet, while side-stepping and circling my magnifying glass.

Violet didn't answer. She was pointing to the door of Mystery Girls HQ.

"Arthur!" she mouthed to me and Poppy.

The door was slightly ajar and I could see Arthur's shoulder through the gap. He was at the top of the rope ladder listening in again! There was only one way to deal with this.

"I JUST DON'T KNOW WHAT WE ARE GOING TO DO!" I said very loudly.

Poppy and Violet gave me a funny look.

"I just don't know what we are going to do about the ghostly guinea pigs EATING people," I said. I had to cover my mouth so I didn't laugh.

"Um, yes. It's JUST AWFUL about that half-chewed human leg we found," Poppy said.

_ha!_

"I am SO scared!" Violet said, putting her hand to her forehead and pretending to faint.

We heard a thud as Arthur dropped to the bottom of the rope ladder. He ran back to the house as if a ghostly guinea pig might actually be chasing him. Having a totally annoying little brother is so much fun sometimes!

Got to go – Miss Crumble might think we've been abducted by ghostly guinea pigs if we are late for school!

Gripped by terror!

12:33 PM
LUNCH TIME, SCHOOL CAFETERIA

At break time we were preparing a plan for
our after-school clue-seeking mission and we
realized something VERY important – the
center of Puddleford has become a hotspot for
paranormal* goings-on. We marked all the
sightings of ghostly guinea pigs so far on a map.

Frankenstein.
VERY PARANORMAL!

(*Paranormal: Means all
things that are spooky)

They have all happened in the center of Puddleford, in a pattern we have called

THE TRIANGLE
OF
SPOOKINESS

The Young Super Sleuth's Handbook says giving memorable names, like **The Library Fine of Fear,** to things that have to do with your mystery makes people take notice of what you are doing.

THE TRIANGLE OF SPOOKINESS sounds so mysterious and exciting that more people might be on the lookout for ghostly guinea pigs. That means more witnesses might come forward with new information to help us solve the case!

4:30 PM
PUDDLEFORD TOWN CENTER

After school today we followed up on the
information from the eyewitnesses by visiting
the locations of the ghostly guinea pig sightings.
The Young Super Sleuth's Handbook says this is a
great way to uncover new clues.

First, we searched every inch of
Miss Crumble's backyard. We'd
never tried to find a ghost
before so we didn't really know
what we were looking for.
Poppy thought maybe there
would be some ghostly slime or
fluff, or something like that.

ghostly
slime

ghostly
fluff

Then we spent ages looking on the floor around Binky's hutch at Roberta's house. After that, we visited the spot where a ghostly guinea pig ran in front of Mr. Drummond's milk truck. All we found there was a smashed milk bottle.

Finally we went over Hazel's garden with a fine toothcomb*. Hazel said if we were going to trample over her vegetables we may as well pull up weeds as we searched for clues. Violet accidentally pulled out Hazel's carrots. We decided it was time to leave after that.

Hazel

*FINE TOOTHCOMB: This isn't actually when you use a comb like the one you use on your hair. It means looking at things really carefully for potential pieces of evidence. It's what a lot of famous detectives in the Young Super Sleuth's Handbook do.

4:50 PM
PUDDLEFORD TOWN CENTER (OUTSIDE PUDDLEFORD THEATER)

We searched everywhere and there was nothing new to report. We needed some ideas about what to do next, so we stopped for a rest outside the theater. A huge banner advertising the talent show was hanging above our heads.

the banner

"I just can't figure out what's attracting the guinea pigs to this part of town," said Violet, studying our map for the fiftieth time today.

I tried to think about things we'd done in the past. What had worked to help us get unstuck when we were stuck?

"We need to get inside their heads," I said. "Remember when we did that with Mom, to help find her missing library books?"

Mom had no idea what had happened to her library books – it was a complete mystery. So, we got her to think back to the day when she last had her books. She had to think really hard but she remembered that she was in a huge rush to finish making Grandma Mystery's birthday present and to get a customer order done.

missing

A to Z of knitting

It turned out Mom had accidentally mailed her library books to Grandma Mystery. We found Grandma Mystery's real birthday present (some stripy pink knitted gloves) at the bottom of Mom's handbag. Mystery solved!

"If you were a ghostly guinea pig, why would you want to hang out around here?" I asked.

Violet pointed to Pampered Pets grooming salon on the map. "Maybe they didn't like going to the pet groomers when they were alive and now they've come back as ghosts to scare pet owners away from the salon?"

"Or they might have guinea pig relatives living in the pet store they want to see?" said Poppy.

I scribbled all the ideas down in my Young Super Sleuth notepad. What Poppy and Violet said could be true. But there were other things that I knew guinea pigs liked to do. Maybe the same things were true of ghostly ones too?

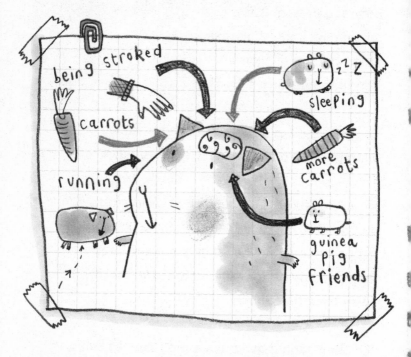

"What if they are staying near the gardens because there are so many vegetables for them to nibble on?" I said. "Although, I don't think ghosts can eat things, can they?"

"You don't think... you don't think they would eat people, do you?" asked Violet.

"Violet, I was only joking when I said that!" I said. I can't believe she actually thinks a guinea pig would eat someone. Also, nobody has been reported missing, so it seems unlikely.

Poppy leaped off the wall. "I know what will help us think of what to do next. Let's do a really, really quick run-through of our dance!"

She jumped into the air and landed in a split, not caring that people walking past were looking at her as if she were crazy. Violet and I pretended to look really busy trying to get inside the ghostly guinea pigs' heads so we didn't have to join in with her.

Beware the human-munching ghostly guinea pigs!

Poppy's detective genius

"Hang on. Mariella, Violet – look at this!" said Poppy. She was pointing to a small heap of little brown lumps next to the basement window of the theater.

"I think it could be guinea pig poo!" she said, looking delighted.

"Poppy! You could be right." I grabbed an evidence bag and some rubber gloves from the Mystery Kit.

We all looked at each other. I knew we were thinking the same thing:

Could these be the **poops** of the ghostly guinea pigs? (And does anyone know if ghosts **poo?**)

5:00 PM
FLUFF 'N' FEATHERS PET STORE,
PUDDLEFORD TOWN CENTER

Next stop was Fluff 'n' Feathers Pet Store. We
needed to speak to a guinea pig expert because
it might help us figure out what was attracting
guinea pigs to the Triangle of Spookiness. Also,
none of us were sure whether the animal droppings
we'd found could have come from a ghost, but we
could check with Mrs. Finn to see if they definitely
did come from a guinea pig.

Local Pet Store

MRS. FINN: Pet store owner who knows loads of stuff about animals. We buy Watson's cat food from her. Hopefully she knows lots about guinea pigs too.

mrs. Finn

I love coming to this pet store. From floor to ceiling, wherever you look, there are different types of pets. Budgies tweeting in a huge glass case, pens with the cutest lop-eared rabbits hopping around in them, hamsters whizzing on their wheels, and glass cases with lizards and snakes, and even one with a ginormous tarantula in it.

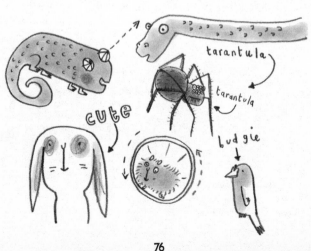

tarantula

tarantula

cute

budgie

In a glass case, underneath the hamsters, the guinea pigs were huddled next to each other on piles of soft fluffy bedding. They were all having what looked like the best afternoon nap ever.

Exhibit A: Cute guinea pigs in fluff 'n' Feathers

hay

guinea pigs!

totally asleep

There were small ones with spiky fur, long-haired ones that are extra cute because it looks like they can't see where they are going, spotty ones, brown ones, and cuddly white ones with pink noses.

DA DAH DEE DAH DUM DAH

DAH DAH DAAAAAAAAAA!

Music blasted into the store.

Violet jumped in shock, Poppy gasped, and I dropped the Mystery Kit. The animals went crazy squeaking and scurrying, and the budgies squawked and flapped around.

Then Mrs. Finn leaped out from what looked like a stock room, her eyes closed in concentration. She pirouetted on one toe, her Fluff 'n' Feathers apron floating in the air as she spun.

Shocked animals

A giant gray poodle wearing a sparkly vest sprang from behind her and landed in her open arms.

In a flash of sequins, he jumped in front of us and started licking Violet's face as if it was a giant dog food-flavored lollipop.

"Arrrgghhheurrgghhhh!"
Violet screamed.

dog food flavored lollipop

Mrs. Finn seemed startled, as though she hadn't been expecting customers today.

"OH, HELLO THERE, HANG ON!" she shouted. She dashed to the back of the store and the music stopped.

Mrs. Finn returned, smoothing her hair and apron into place. "Spangle and I were just getting a bit of practice in before the big day. Only two days left until the talent show!"

costume ENVY

Poppy was gazing at Spangle's costume. "Two days!" she said. "How am I going to finish our costumes in two days?"

Violet was laughing as she struggled to stop Spangle from licking her.

Honestly, had everyone forgotten why we were here? Our top priority was to ask Mrs. Finn questions about the case.

"Could we ask you a few questions, Mrs. Finn? We are investigating something quite strange that's going on in Puddleford," I said, taking charge of the situation.

Mrs Finn peered at me. "Ah, Mariella, it's you, dear. I didn't recognize you there. How's the cat? Watson, isn't it?"

"He's still got a thing for scratching the wallpaper, but apart from that he's fine," I replied. "Mrs. Finn, have you heard about the strange things that have been happening – with guinea pigs?"

"Guinea pigs? Heavens, no!" Mrs. Finn said, fixing a sticker to the case with the budgies in. It said "chinchillas for sale." That was a bit weird. Surely a pet store owner would know the difference?

WEIRD

CHINCHILLAS for SALE

When we told Mrs. Finn what had been going on, she was shocked. She had been totally focused on preparing for the talent show and hadn't seen any of the posters we had put up around town.

I showed her the evidence bag containing the suspected guinea pig poops.

"Mrs. Finn," I said. "Do you think these poops could have come from a guinea pig?"

She examined the bag closely. "Yes, girls, I think these look very much as though they could be guinea pig droppings."

"We need to let you know to stay alert," I said, "Ghostly guinea pigs are active in this area.

Your pet shop is at the center of the Triangle of Spookiness and we found these poops outside the theater, just around the corner."

"Crumbs!" said Mrs. Finn.

Mrs. Finn said she would keep a look-out for anything strange and she offered to tell us everything she knows about guinea pigs to help us solve the mystery.

"Guinea pigs come in lots of different shapes and sizes," she said, gesturing toward the hamster enclosure.

"Um, I think those are hamsters," Poppy said politely.

Mrs. Finn peered into the case, almost sticking her entire face in there. "Oh yes, so they are. Silly me!"

Mrs. Finn reached into the guinea pig case and pulled out three. She passed us one each. They were the cutest things I'd ever seen.

fluffy

"I call this one Fluffy, because of his hair," Mrs. Finn said about the gray guinea pig Poppy was holding. Fluffy's hair sticks up on end in loads of different directions. It's a bit like Dad's hair first thing in the morning.

"And this is Goldilocks," Mrs. Finn said, stroking the head of the guinea pig with long flowing silky fur that Violet was holding. "She needs lots of grooming to keep her coat in tip-top condition."

Goldilocks

"**Achoo!**" Violet sneezed. She is allergic to most things. It looks like guinea pigs are one of them.

"This is one of my favorites. I call him Mischief. He's got so much personality," Mrs. Finn continued, tickling the ear of the snoozing brown-and-white guinea pig in my arms.

"This type of breed is really popular. His nice short coat is easy to take care of."

I could see why. Mischief really was SO cute.

"Right, now let me think. What else can I tell you about guinea pigs?" said Mrs. Finn thoughtfully.

I balanced Mischief on my knee and grabbed my pencil and Young Super Sleuth notebook ...

GUINEA PIG FACTS

DIFFERENT BREEDS OF GUINEA PIG:

Peruvian

Sheltie

Abyssinian

Rex

Short haired

FAVORITE FOODS: Dandelions, grass, guinea pig nibbles, broccoli, and carrots. Any vegetables really. (There are no recorded cases of a guinea pig eating a human, ever.)

SLEEPING HABITS: Guinea pigs need six hours of sleep a day. They are active both at night and during the day.

asleep

POOPS: Guinea pig poops are small sausage-shaped pellets, like the ones we found outside the theater.

POOPS

AGILITY: Guinea pigs can move quickly. Mrs. Finn sometimes has trouble catching them when customers want to buy one.

fast!

BEHAVIOR: In the wild, guinea pigs live and make their nests in burrows. They communicate through different types of squeaks. They are sociable animals and live in colonies of up to twenty.

SQUEAK

nest?

burrow

5:20 PM
STILL AT FLUFF 'N' FEATHERS

Mrs. Finn disappeared into the back of the store
for ages, saying she had something urgent to
attend to. When she came back she was holding
a tray of teeny little cupcakes.

"The guinea pigs love them," she said.

She showed us a stand filled with her special pet
treats. There were meaty-flavored bone-shaped
cakes for dogs, little fish-shaped tuna
and prawn buns for cats, and seed
clusters for the budgies that looked a
bit like miniature flapjacks.

Mrs. Finn opened the case and put the guinea pig cupcakes inside. The guinea pigs must have caught a whiff of the treats because they all started to wake up.

We put Fluffy, Goldilocks, and Mischief back in the case, and they were wriggling all over the place, trying to get to the cupcakes.

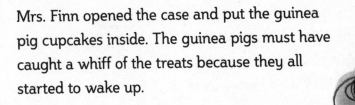

Fluff

They were so desperate to eat them that they were swallowing them whole.

Mrs. Finn just looked on smiling. "Ah, you see, it's nice how they all share, isn't it?"

How was she missing that it looked like there was a guinea pig wrestling match in the pen? The guinea pigs were going crazy over the seed cupcakes.

"ACHOO!" Violet sneezed. "Excuse me, I think I might be allergic to – **ACHOO!** – allergic to guinea pigs!"

Fur and fluff was rising from
their pen, making Violet's
sneezing attack worse. We
decided we'd better leave.
Mrs. Finn gave us a bag of
fishy tuna treats for Watson.
That gave me an idea. The guinea
pigs in the pet store loved the treats
so much – maybe they would tempt
a ghostly guinea pig too? We still aren't sure
whether ghosts actually eat things but it's worth
a try. Mrs. Finn gave us some of the dandelion
and burdock seed treats to use as bait to try and
catch a ghostly guinea pig.

FlUFF !

"Good luck solving the mystery!"
Mrs. Finn called as she launched into
another dance rehearsal with Spangle.
She spun toward the back of the store,
knocking over a pile of dog food cans
as she went.

POOP

5:30 PM
PUDDLEFORD TOWN CENTER (OUTSIDE THE PICKLED PEPPER CAFÉ)

"It was a great idea to go and see Mrs. Finn, Violet," I said. "I'm surprised she got all the right ingredients in her pet treats though."

"What do you mean?" said Violet.

I knew it! Poppy and Violet had been so distracted by the cuteness of the guinea pigs they'd stopped looking for clues.

"Mrs. Finn couldn't see what she was doing," I said. "She was banging into things and getting all the animals mixed up. I think she needs to get some glasses."

"I thought she was just distracted. With the talent show coming up, it's so hard to concentrate," said Poppy.

ARRRGGGHHH!

Never mind the talent show! I can't concentrate on anything else besides the ghostly guinea pigs!

Poppy needs to stop thinking about tap shoes!

5:45 PM
OUTSIDE PUDDLEFORD THEATER (AGAIN)

We laid a trap outside the theater using an empty box of dog food from the pet store and the treats from Mrs. Finn. We're going to go back tomorrow morning.

"Come on, we've still got time to squeeze in another talent show practice before we have to go home," said Poppy.

"I suppose we can't do anything else now. We've just got to wait for a ghostly guinea pig to discover those treats," I said. (And the talent show is tomorrow and I totally don't know what I'm supposed to be doing.)

box

twig

treats

"I wonder if ... **ACHOO!** I wonder if I'm allergic to ghostly guinea pigs too?" Violet said.

"I hope not! If we catch a ghostly guinea pig, I was hoping we could use it as a prop for our talent show act," said Poppy cheerfully.

I think Poppy was joking. If we find a ghostly guinea pig in our trap we need to investigate what on earth it's doing there, not use it to win the talent show. (Although if we did win, that would be quite cool because loads more people would know who the Mystery Girls are and we'd get loads more big cases like this.)

The WORLD Famous MYSTERY GIRLS

Violet Maple

mariella mystery

poppy Holmes

SATURDAY
April 8th

DETECTIVE FACT: Detectives drink loads of coffee so they can stay awake all night solving cases. (I saw it in a detective film.)

coffee →

Mom says I'm too young to drink coffee (yeah, right!), but I've used Dad's mug to make this page look like a real detective's diary.

Huge

me

3:15 AM
22 SYCAMORE AVENUE (MY BEDROOM)

I just woke up and the WEIRDEST thing happened.
I was having a dream that I was being chased by
a huge ghostly guinea pig. I couldn't escape from
it because I was wearing giant tap dancing shoes.
Just before the ghostly guinea pig was about to
eat me, I woke up.

I was trying to get back to sleep – that's when I
noticed it. There, on the top of my Young Super
Sleuth notebook, the bag of suspected ghostly
guinea pig poops was glowing in the dark! I guess
that answers the question about whether or not
ghosts can poo!

I tried waking up Mom and Dad, but they said a bag
of poo did not justify being woken up at 3 am.

If I had a flashlight I could send coded signals to
Poppy and Violet: "HELP, GLOWING GHOSTLY
POO IN MY ROOM!" I can't see their houses from
where I live, though, so they would have to move
closer for that to work.

I put the bag of glowing poops in a drawer.
They are spooking me out a bit. To distract myself,
I've written down a list of things I need to do
in the morning:

1. Check if ghostly guinea pig poos still glow.

2. Remind Mom and Dad that they are my
parents and as such they need to be prepared
to support my mystery solving around the clock.

3. Check that my tap shoes are
definitely the right size.

8:30 AM
22 SYCAMORE AVENUE (STILL MY HOUSE)

I got up this morning and went straight to grab the bag of ghostly poops. They were still glowing in the drawer. But when I pulled the bag into the light, they looked totally normal, not glowing or ghostly at all. Weird.

glowing

I rushed downstairs. I didn't have time to stop
and untangle Watson from the yarn he was
wrapped in. Or to wonder why he was covered
in potato peelings.

watson

Potato
Peelings?

In the kitchen, Dad was making toast and Mom
was fiddling with a hat in the shape of a carrot on
Arthur's head. (More novelty hats – great.)

"What was all that fuss about in the middle of the
night?" Mom asked.

"I was trying to show you and Dad this," I said,
holding up the evidence bag. "They look like
normal poops now, but look what happens when
you put them in the dark."

Mom made a face as I put the bag in an empty biscuit tin. Mom and Dad took turns peeking under the lid at the glowing poops. They were baffled too.

glowing POO

"Ooooooh! Let me have a look," said Arthur.

"Are you sure you should, darling?" asked Mom. "I don't want you to get scared about the ghostly guinea pigs again."

"I'm not scared of them," Arthur said, grabbing the biscuit tin and peeking in as if the poops might leap out and attack him. He totally *is* scared.

"You might want to have a look at this, Mariella." Dad said, passing me the *Puddleford Gazette*. "We decided to run a special feature on the Ghostly Guinea Pigs of Puddleford. The Mystery Girls get a special mention."

Ooh, we're famous!

THE BEASTS OF PUDDLEFORD

There have been reports of strange creatures on the loose in Puddleford. A series of eyewitnesses claim to have seen what appear to be glowing green guinea pigs. The creatures have been referred to as "ghostly guinea pigs" by young local mystery solvers, the Mystery Girls.

People who have seen a ghostly guinea pig are understandably shaken by the experience. "The talent show is coming up in a few days and I feel really nervous about going out after dark," says Roberta Poppet, aged eight, who saw a ghostly guinea pig in her backyard.

Artist's impression of a ghostly guinea pig:

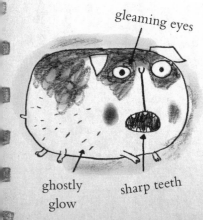

gleaming eyes

ghostly glow

sharp teeth

ROBERTA POPPET

Some seem to have had more terrifying experiences than others. We spoke to Mrs. Pavlova, local cat enthusiast, about the creature she saw. "I couldn't believe my eyes.

MRS. PAVLOVA

There it was, growling at me on top of my garbage cans. It had gleaming green eyes and razor sharp teeth. And I think it had huge claws too. If I hadn't flung a bag of potato peelings at the beast, I probably wouldn't be standing here now."

Advice from the Puddleford Council is to remain calm. If you see one of these creatures, do not approach it. Call the police, who are on standby to deal with any incidents of unusual animal behavior.

I'm not sure Mrs. Pavlova from across the street actually saw a ghostly guinea pig. Watson rubbed up against my leg. Hmmm. "What have you been up to?" I said, narrowing my eyes. He still had slimy potato peelings stuck in his collar.

"Whass bowing on with dem?" said Arthur, his mouth full of food. In his hand was the bag of treats Mrs. Finn had given us for Watson.

"Arthur! Do you realize you are eating cat food?" I said. Ha. Served him right.

Arthur looked horrified and ran to the bathroom. In his panic he scattered the bag of cat treats on the floor and Watson pounced on them, sucking them up like we never feed him anything. Those pet treats must be good – hopefully good enough to attract a ghostly guinea pig into our trap!

9:30 AM
ON THE WAY TO PUDDLEFORD THEATER

I took the ghostly poops to show Poppy and Violet.

"Whoa! Look at this, Violet!" said Poppy, holding out the biscuit tin.

"Oh my goodness! They really do glow!" Violet gasped. "If the guinea pigs look as ghostly as their poops it's no wonder the eyewitnesses are scared."

"And can you believe we're on the front page of the *Gazette*?" I said.

glowing poop

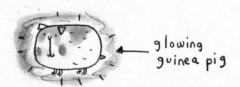

glowing guinea pig

"With that and our talent show appearance, everybody will know how wonderful we are at solving mysteries!" said Poppy.

I hope Poppy is right, but there is still A LOT of work to do.

We reached the theater and peered down the alley at the side. Something, maybe a ghostly guinea pig, had disturbed the trap!

This could be the moment, I thought. The moment when we discover a real ghostly guinea pig.

"It's vitally important that we don't let the ghostly guinea pig escape – if there is one inside the box, that is," I whispered.

crumbs (treats gone)

twig

"Mariella, I don't like this," Violet said, clutching my shoulder.

"I think I should lift the box," said Poppy. "You two have no coordination. You might set free whatever is under there."

"Great idea," said Violet, shoving Poppy forward.

Poppy kneeled on the floor next to the trap and, very slowly, lifted up the box. "I can't see anything. Hang on, what's that?"

"What? What is it?" I said. Violet was squeezing my shoulder so tightly it was starting to hurt.

"Oh. Bad news," said Poppy. "All I can see is some crumbs from the seed cupcake treats."

"This isn't all bad," said Violet. "The seed cupcakes have gone, and look, the box has been nibbled at the side. That tells us some sort of creature was here last night."

"But we can't say for sure it was a ghostly guinea pig," I said.

I couldn't help but feel disappointed. Violet was right, the box had been nibbled, but we were still no closer to catching an actual ghostly guinea pig, or solving the case.

"Look at this," Poppy said, pointing to another pile of small brown lumps. "More poo!"

"Great! You are getting really good at finding clues, Poppy," I said, feeling better. "Especially poo-related ones."

Wearing the gloves from the Mystery Kit, I scooped up the poo and put it in the biscuit tin.

gloves

"Wow! It glows, it's more ghostly poo," I said.

"That means it **was** a ghostly guinea pig that nibbled its way out of our trap," said Violet.

"We need to come back tonight," I said. "The Young Super Sleuth's Handbook says a surveillance trip is a good idea when you have gathered enough evidence, and we've got loads of evidence now!"

"I'm not sure about this, girls," Violet said, looking worried.

"OK, we're going to need more guinea pig treats from Mrs. Finn," said Poppy, ignoring Violet. "And PLEASE can we have a dress rehearsal before we go out on surveillance? The talent show is tonight!"

I need to stay calm. It's just a surveillance trip to try and solve the most important mystery we've ever had about some totally weird ghosts who can eat, poo, and chew their way out of boxes. And a talent show in front of the whole town of Puddleford – **arrgggghhhhhh!**

under
surveillance

10:15 AM
FLUFF 'N' FEATHERS PET STORE

Mrs. Finn was brushing
Spangle's ears when we
arrived at the pet store.
(His fur is kind of like
my hair, wild and
curly.)

She was delighted when she heard how much
the guinea pigs and Watson had enjoyed her
treats. She packed us a box of supplies, saying
we should take whatever we needed to get to the
bottom of this.

I peeked into the case of guinea pigs. They were
fast asleep. There was no sign that the seed cupcake
chaos ever happened.

"Aww, look at Fluffy," said Poppy, pointing to a large gray lump underneath some hay.

"Where's Goldilocks?" gasped Violet. "She hasn't been sold, has she?" (Trust Violet to have a favorite guinea pig even though she's completely allergic to them.)

"Don't worry, she's just there," said Mrs. Finn. She was pointing to an enormous long-haired blonde guinea pig who looked as if she'd eaten a few too many of Mrs. Finn's treats, and possibly Goldilocks too.

not goldilocks

"And there's Mischief's little bottom's sticking out of the hay!" Mrs. Finn smiled.

I don't remember Mischief having a black patch on his bottom, or that gigantic guinea pig being there yesterday.

"Mrs. Finn, have you sold any guinea pigs since we last saw you? There seem to be a few missing – and some new ones too," I said.

hay

"Some of them will be hiding under that pile of hay," said Mrs. Finn. "Now, I hope you don't mind but I need to close the store early. Spangle and I are going to spend the afternoon doing a dress rehearsal for tonight's show."

"That's a very good idea, Mrs. Finn," said Poppy, flashing me and Violet a serious look. "Dress rehearsals are VERY important, aren't they, girls?"

11:00 AM
MYSTERY GIRLS HQ

"There's no way that was Goldilocks," said Violet as we walked away from the pet store.

"I don't think that was Mischief either," I said.

"What's going on? If that wasn't Mischief and Goldilocks, what happened to them?" said Poppy.

"This could be very important," I said, grabbing my Young Super Sleuth notebook. "What could the logical explanations be?"

Logical Explanation One: Goldilocks and Mischief were hiding under the pile of hay today, with lots of the other guinea pigs.

This could be true. But the pile of hay didn't look that big.

(Sort of) Logical Explanation Two:

The giant guinea pig Mrs. Finn thinks is Goldilocks has eaten some of the guinea pigs.

Violet is pretty sure guinea pigs don't eat each other. (I think she still needs convincing that ghostly guinea pigs don't eat humans, though.)

(Weird, but Possibly True) Logical Explanation Three: Goldilocks and Mischief have been kidnapped by the ghostly guinea pigs.

That might not be true but it's definitely too much of a coincidence that there are unexplained ghostly guinea pigs running around town AND guinea pigs disappearing from the pet store. From now on Fluff 'n' Feathers is under surveillance.

5:00 PM
MYSTERY GIRLS HQ (PREPARING FOR SURVEILLANCE TRIP)

Two hours until the talent show starts. Our final rehearsal didn't go too badly. I only tripped over twice and Violet managed to perfect smiling and swaying really well. Poppy has decided that Violet and I will be more like back-up dancers who stand still most of the time. I don't know why we didn't think of it sooner.

Our dancing might not be great but our costumes are REALLY good. I don't know where Poppy found the time to finish them with everything that's happened this week. We look like real detectives in raincoats and fedora hats. The fake moustaches and sparkly tap shoes finish off the look wonderfully.

totally AMAZING

sparkly tap shoes

fedora hat

fake moustaches

rain coat

We have a big evening ahead of us. There are some very important things to do:

1. VISIT GHOSTLY GUINEA PIG HOTSPOTS IN **THE TRIANGLE OF SPOOKINESS**: Keep watch for ghostly guinea pigs at the theater and the other places ghostly guinea pigs have been spotted. (We are allowed to stay out late tonight for the talent show, so we need to do as much as possible.)

2. KEEP THE PET STORE UNDER SURVEILLANCE: No ghostly guinea pigs have been spotted here, but we can't rule out that the ghostly guinea pigs might have something to do with the disappearance of Mrs. Finn's guinea pigs.

3. GET TO THE BOTTOM OF THE GUINEA PIG MADNESS: It's a big task, but the Mystery Girls can do it.

4. AMAZE THE AUDIENCE AT THE TALENT SHOW WITH OUR DANCING DETECTIVES ACT: Winning first place, becoming famous beyond our wildest dreams. (Poppy made me write that, she's obsessed!)

Before we left on our surveillance mission we did a quick test to make sure Poppy's Young Super Sleuth walkie-talkies worked.

"Do you read me, Popsicle?" I said to Poppy. (We're using undercover code names for this mission.)

"Reading you loud and clear, Mariell-Star. Vi-vacious, do you copy?" Poppy replied.

"I can hear you both fine, but I am sitting right next to you," said Violet.

We also checked that the Mystery Kit had all the supplies we needed:

walkie-talkie

Mystery Kit Supplies

Young Super Sleuth's Handbook.

Fishing net

Box with some hay in it (for a ghostly guinea pig if we catch one)

THE YOUNG SUPER SLEUTH'S HANDBOOK ?

THE YOUNG SUPER SLEUTHS

Camera (to try and capture a picture of a ghostly guinea pig)

Potato chips (in case we get hungry)

SALT and Vinegar

Newspapers, to hide behind and look inconspicuous (Blending in, so nobody notices us)

Carrots

PUDDLEFORD GAZETTE

Dandelion seed cupcakes

"Right, Poppy, you and Violet keep watch over the alley at the side of the theater. I'll do a sweep* of the Triangle of Spookiness, then we'll meet at the pet store."

*The Young Super Sleuth's Handbook says it's important to do a "sweep" of any areas linked to your mystery — it's not like sweeping the floor: you look really carefully for more clues, or in this case a ghostly guinea pig.

sweep

THE SURVEILLANCE TRIP

(still Saturday April 8th)

Our surveillance trip was TOTALLY crazy – this is an accurate account of what happened after we left Mystery Girls HQ (at 5:17 pm).

SECRET AGENT Mariell-Star
★ ★ ★
AKA Mariella Mystery
TOP SECRET

THE UNDERCOVER MISSION: SURVEILLANCE

Many mysteries can only be solved by "going undercover." This involves being inconspicuous and gathering clues without anybody noticing what you are doing.

Undercover Essentials ...

You may need to wear a **disguise** to protect your true identity. This could include wearing large sunglasses, a hat, or a fake beard.

Hello, Mr. Sparklepants speaking ...

To make sure nobody knows who you are or what you are doing, you should work under a **false name**.

Keep a **hidden camera** on you at all times to capture important evidence.

Beauty mark camera

Flower camera

Beard camera

Handbag camera

Discover Famous Detectives

Marcelle du Wimpelle was a master of disguise. He managed to capture art thieves who had evaded the police for years by posing as an old lady who was hard of hearing. When the art thieves tried to steal a priceless statue, Marcelle took them by surprise.

Harmless old lady one minute, elite art-thief catcher the next. Can you make your disguise as convincing as Marcelle's?

5:45 PM
THE TRIANGLE OF SPOOKINESS

Tap shoes weren't the best shoes to wear for an undercover mission. You could hear me coming from miles away.

Clip clop, clip clop.

DESERTED!

weird shadow!

GARDENS

The gardens were deserted. I deduced everyone had headed to the theater for the talent show. It was just me. All on my own.

My walkie-talkie crackled and made me jump. "Mariell-Star, do you copy?" said Poppy.

"I can hear you, Popsicle. Anything to report? It's all quiet at the gardens," I replied.

"We've had to abandon our surveillance of the theater, Mariell-Star!" Poppy said.

What? We had a plan!

SPOOKY!

"The theater is really busy with people arriving for the talent show," said Violet. "We haven't got any chance of seeing a ghostly guinea pig with all the noise."

"Good thinking," I said. I really did know that I could rely on them. "Go to the pet store and see if anything is going on there. I still need to check out the other hotspots in the Triangle."

"Be careful, Mariell-Star," said Violet.

Leaving the gardens, I walked around the back of Roberta's house. It was really quiet, spookily quiet. All I could hear was the sound of my tap shoes.

CliP Clop   ClipClop

No sign of ghostly guinea pig activity. I decided to check in with the others again.

"Popsicle, Vi-Vacious, anything to report?"

The walkie-talkie crackled, then Poppy said, "We haven't seen anything unusual yet. Hang on. Mrs. Finn is leaving the store with Spangle. She's dressed in her costume. Is that a cape she's wearing?"

"Go in for a closer look. Can you see through the window of the pet store?" I said.

"Mariell-Star!" Violet's voice crackled through the walkie-talkie. "Goldilocks is in the building. I repeat, we can see Goldilocks."

"Vi-Vacious, is Mischief there?"

"No sign of Mischief or Fluffy. In fact, there are hardly any guinea pigs at all. I can only see five," Violet said.

But the pet store has been closed since lunchtime. Mrs. Finn couldn't have sold any guinea pigs. So where were they?!

"Popsicle, Vi-Vacious – this confirms our suspicions. The pet store guinea pigs definitely have something to do with the ghostly guinea pigs," I said. "Stay where you are, I'm coming!"

I found Poppy and Violet standing across the street from the pet store. They were being inconspicuous behind their newspapers. I whipped out my newspaper and stood next to them.

Inconspicous

We could have just been three people reading the paper – you'd never know we were actually on the lookout for a ghostly guinea pig.

"Nothing else to report," said Poppy, under her breath. "I'm sure something will happen soon though."

A figure dashed around the corner. It was Miss Crumble.

"Hi, girls! Don't you look fabulous in your costumes!" she said. (I think maybe our disguises needed more work.)

"Are you OK, Miss Crumble? You haven't seen anything else strange, have you?" said Violet.

"Oh, I'll be fine. I've been keeping an eye out for Mr. Darcy, but so far I haven't seen him again. I am in a rush to get a good seat at the talent show though," she said. "Shouldn't you all be at the theater by now?"

Poppy looked at her watch nervously. I explained to Miss Crumble that we were undercover, trying to locate Mr. Darcy and his ghostly friends. Miss Crumble pulled her jacket collar up and looked along the empty street.

tick tock

"Good luck, girls, I hope you get to the bottom of this." Then she hurried away to the theater and everything was quiet again.

We stood there for what felt like ages and ages. Nothing happened.

"It's getting late," said Poppy. "I'd really like to stay but we can't miss our slot on stage."

"Let's just take one last look in the window and check that nothing weird is happening," I said. I didn't want to give up just yet.

We set off across the street, the clip-clopping of our shoes echoing down the empty street.

"Stop," Poppy whispered suddenly. "Can you hear that?"

There was a rustling noise coming from behind a row of garbage cans in the alleyway, next to the pet groomers. We all held our breath.

I reached in my pocket for the camera. Was this the moment we were going to see a real, live ghostly guinea pig?

The lid of one of the cans rattled. A shadow moved.

Violet made a whimpering noise. Then, rising from among the rubbish, we saw a huge, dark figure. It started staggering toward us …

"AAAAAArrrggHHHHhhhhHHhh!"

Dark and mysterious shadow...

I closed my eyes and pointed the camera at the garbage cans, hoping to catch a picture of the ghostly guinea pig before I ran for my life.

"Don't leave meeeeeeeee!" a terrified voice called after us.

Hang on, I thought. I know that voice.

I turned to see Arthur shuffling toward us, dressed in a bright orange knitted carrot costume.

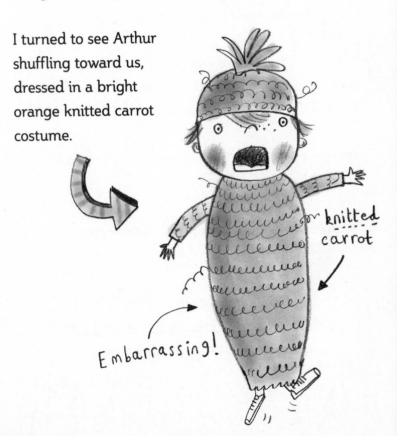

knitted carrot

Embarrassing!

Unbelievable.

This is exactly why he can't be a Mystery Girl.

"WHAT are you doing here?" I demanded.

"I wanted to help you find the ghostly guinea pigs! Mom thinks I'm backstage at the talent show," Arthur said.

"Arthur, if there were any ghostly guinea pigs nearby, you've managed to scare them all off," I sighed. "And why are you dressed as a carrot?"

"It's part of my act," Arthur beamed. "I'm doing a special happy carrot dance."

So that was why he was wearing the carrot hat this morning.

"You do know that carrots are the second favorite food of ghostly guinea pigs, don't you?" I said, "After humans, that is."

"You're lying. I know you are because I looked in your Young Super Sleuth journal. It said in there that ghostly guinea pigs definitely didn't eat people!" Arthur said, folding his arms.

"I ... what ... you've been in Mystery Girls HQ again!" I said, furious. There is top secret and **VERY** private information in this journal.

Just then one of our *Have You Seen This Ghostly Guinea Pig?* posters fluttered past in the wind, landing in a muddy puddle.

What's the point? I thought. The mission was a disaster. I'd always be a bad detective, probably with a giant carrot as a sidekick.

"Come on. We should get to the theater," said Poppy, breaking the silence.

"ACHoo! ACHOO! ACHOoOooO!" Violet started having one of her sneezing fits again. She must be allergic to Arthur's knitted costume.

Poppy and I searched through the Mystery Kit trying to find her a tissue.

"Um, Mariella," Arthur said, pulling on the sleeve of my coat. I ignored him.

"It's OK, I'll ... ACHOO! ACHOO! I'll be OK. ACHOO!" Violet spluttered.

"Empty everything out," said Poppy. "I'm sure there's a tissue in here somewhere."

"Mariella," Arthur whispered. "You need to look at this."

"Look at what? Can't you see we're busy?" I snapped.

"You need to look at the ghostly guinea pig, over there, by the lamp post," Arthur squeaked.

I froze. There, sitting on a patch of grass outside the pet store, glowing eerily in the fading daylight, a small ghostly guinea pig was munching on a dandelion.

"Mr. Darcy," breathed Violet.

An actual ghostly guinea pig. Crazy.

TRACKING A SUSPECT:

Getting to the point where you have the suspect in your sights is very rewarding: you could be about to solve your mystery. Follow the Young Super Sleuth simple guidelines to make sure you don't let your suspect get away.

Young Super Sleuth Tracking Guidelines

Remain calm – under no circumstances make any sudden movements or loud noises. This could alert your suspect to the fact they are being followed.

Silent tip toe

Keep a **camera** handy – if you can catch your suspect "red handed" and photograph it, your case could be solved.

If your suspect is moving, **follow them** calmly and thoughtfully. Use lamp posts or other objects to conceal yourself from view.

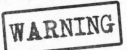

WARNING

Try to avoid chase situations. A chase almost always results in the suspect getting away.

REMAIN SENSIBLE: Always let an adult know if you are going to be tracking a suspect, especially if the suspect is a known criminal. Good luck!

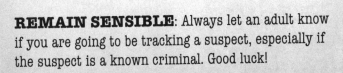

6:42 PM
OUTSIDE FLUFF 'N' FEATHERS PET STORE
(WITH A GHOSTLY GUINEA PIG)

We all stood still for what seemed like ages. The ghostly guinea pig (who matched Miss Crumble's description of Mr. Darcy) carried on nibbling his dandelion leaf. I could see what the eyewitnesses meant – Mr. Darcy was giving off a totally eerie green glow.

"I'm going to see if I can get close to him," I whispered. "Poppy, get ready with the net. Violet, pass me those guinea pig treats."

"Mariella, it's glowing!" said Violet.

I was getting worried about Violet. Was everyone ten minutes behind here?

"I know, Maple, now pass me those guinea pig treats!" (In high-stress situations, detectives sometimes call each other by their last names. It shows you mean business.)

"Be careful!" wailed Arthur, his hands over his eyes.

terrified!

I stepped forward, trying not to make any sudden movements.

Clip clop ...

Arrrgggghhhh! The tap shoes.

Clip clop ...

Mr. Darcy's ears twitched.

Clip clop ...

Mr. Darcy made a break for it, moving at lightning speed. It looked as if he was flying across the road. Well, he is a ghost, after all.

"GET HIM!" I shouted.

Mr. Darcy dashed in the direction of the theater. We sprinted after him.

The ticket attendant stepped out of the doors in front of us and we went straight into him. "Oooopppphhh! Watch where you're going!" he groaned, rubbing his leg. "You're cutting it close; the show starts in five minutes."

"Oh my goodness, he's right!" said Poppy.

"The guinea pig. We were chasing a guinea pig!" I gasped, looking around desperately for Mr. Darcy. I couldn't see him anywhere.

The ticket attendant obviously thought we'd gone crazy. "You all need to be backstage immediately or you'll miss your slot," he said.

"Oh no!" Arthur cried. "I'm opening the show!"

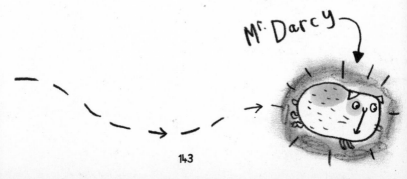

Mr. Darcy

6:55 PM
PUDDLEFORD THEATER (TRACKING MR. DARCY)

I looked down the alleyway at the side of the theater. Nothing. We needed to act quickly.

"Mr. Darcy could be in the building somewhere. Let's get searching," I said to the others.

"**ACHOO!**" said Violet.

Violet's sneezing! I had a moment of detective genius. I didn't know why I hadn't thought of it before.

"Violet, I think you are allergic to ghostly guinea pigs. You couldn't stop sneezing when we were near Mr. Darcy. Maybe your sneezes can lead us to the guinea pigs?"

Violet's nose!

"You're a genius, Mariella!" said Poppy. Had she only just noticed?

"We've got twenty minutes before we're on stage. Let's catch that ghostly guinea pig," Poppy said, straightening our fedora hats.

There was hardly any room to move – there
were so many people preparing to go on stage,
getting their costumes ready and putting the
last-minute touches to their act.

Mrs. Finn was getting Spangle to jump through a
hoop covered in glittering gems. A lady wearing
a giant pink beehive wig was humming to herself,
and a troupe of five-year-olds in tutus
was being taken through a very
uncoordinated dance. (Even
their dancing looked better
than mine and Violet's.)

A flustered lady wearing a microphone headset marched over to Arthur waving her clipboard. "Arthur Mystery? You need to get on stage NOW. The curtain is about to go up!"

Arthur shuffled after her toward the black curtain at the side of the stage.

The lady with the clipboard had to help him up the stairs because he couldn't bend his legs in his carrot costume. Just before he disappeared behind the curtain, he turned and gave us a thumbs-up. How embarrassing. I hoped nobody realized I was with the giant carrot.

We continued to scan the floor for Mr. Darcy, edging past a lady who was trying to squeeze her very bendy body into a very small box.

bendy "!"

We turned a corner into a narrow, deserted corridor. There were parts of lighting equipment piled everywhere. We tiptoed (not very quietly in the tap shoes) further along.

"What's that?" whispered Violet. "Look over there."

Something was glowing, very faintly, on the floor.

"Footprints," Poppy said, whipping out her magnifying glass. "Little glowing footprints!"

Weird, I thought. Not only do these ghosts eat, poop, and trigger allergic reactions. Now they leave footprints.

"Let's follow them!" I whispered. "I bet they will lead us to Mr. Darcy. Violet, how does your nose feel?"

"It's definitely tickling a bit. We must be going the right way," said Violet.

A red light flickered on the wall behind us. A sign said: QUIET PLEASE, PERFORMANCE IN PROGRESS.

Violet let out an enormous sneeze. "ACHOO!"

Suddenly, the lights went out, plunging us into darkness. Violet gripped my shoulder.

"Don't worry. I think the show is about to start. Let's keep going!" I whispered.

The footprints glowed even brighter as we followed them around another corner. I couldn't really see where we were going. My tap shoe caught on something. I grabbed hold of Poppy and heard Violet screech. I felt myself stumble and fall, then something brushed against my face and we landed in a tangled heap in the darkness.

"My hands! I can't see my hands!" Violet squeaked.

It really was dark. Had we fallen into a cabinet or a mysterious world that only ghostly guinea pigs live in? I couldn't believe I'd forgotten to pack a flashlight in the Mystery Kit.

I felt around on the floor for something that might tell us where we were. My hand brushed against something hairy. A ghostly guinea pig? No. It was just my fake moustache. Phew.

A bright light clicked on, shining in our eyes. I blinked and saw Arthur standing in front of us, looking puzzled. I looked to the side and saw that Poppy's fake moustache had come unstuck at one end and Violet had landed on her hat, flattening it.

"Don't make any sudden movements," breathed Poppy.

"Why? What's going on?" wailed Violet, shielding her eyes.

"I think we're on the stage – we're the opening act!" said Poppy, leaping to her feet.

"LADEEEZ AND GENTLEMEN!"
the talent show host boomed. "Please
welcome on stage, Arthur Carrot and …
the Mystery Girls! Who, strictly speaking, aren't
on stage until later on … but put your hands
together anyway!"

The audience clapped and music began to play.
Arthur looked at us, shrugged his shoulders and
began to dance, waving his arms around and
shaking his bottom.

He jumped over the Mystery Kit. I must have
dropped it when we fell. The box of guinea pig
treats had spilled right across the stage.

Then Poppy stood up and started to join in with
Arthur's dance. It was the most embarrassing thing
that has ever happened in my entire life.

mystery kit

There was nothing else to do. We had to smile and sway like we'd practiced earlier. Poppy winked at us and got out her magnifying glass. She pretended to be examining Arthur's carrot costume, chasing him around the stage. The audience thought this was hilarious.

Violet and I joined in. We ended up making a sort of conga line, kicking our legs out and waving our hats.

When the music came to an end, everyone cheered and whooped.

Come to think of it, maybe it wasn't so embarrassing after all. They loved us!

treats

Suddenly there was a scream from the audience.

"AAARRRGGGHH!
GHOSTLY GUINEA PIGS!"

I looked around the stage. A ghostly guinea pig
was nibbling the edge of Arthur's costume.
Mr. Darcy hadn't got away after all!

I spotted a cluster of them peeking their noses out
from underneath the Reach for the Stars Talent
Show sign. More and more were appearing from
under the curtain at the back of the stage. They
were trying to get to the spilled guinea pig treats!

I made an emergency deduction – Puddleford
Theater was being invaded by ghostly guinea pigs!

7:08 PM
PUDDLEFORD THEATER
(DEFINITE GHOSTLY GUINEA PIG HOTSPOT)

Within seconds the whole audience was out of their seats, screeching and screaming. Arthur was wailing helplessly as the ghostly guinea pig chewed his giant carrot costume.

Somebody screamed,

"Save US! It's the BEASTS OF PUDDLEFORD!"

The stage lights came on and little flashes of fur scurried for cover. Immediately the guinea pigs vanished again. All except the guinea pig eating Arthur's costume, who stayed still just long enough for us to get a good look at him.

"That's not a ghostly guinea pig! That's Mischief, from the pet store," I said, as his furry bottom darted behind the curtains.

mischief!

"STAY CALM, PLEASE, FOLKS. JUST A SLIGHT TECHNICAL HITCH!" the talent show host was saying, his voice shaking. "Our next act on stage is Mrs. Marjorie Finn and Spangle the Wonder Dog!"

Mrs. Finn's music began to play and we heard a cheerful bark from Spangle. Poor Mrs. Finn, having to go on stage while the audience was terrified about being attacked by ghostly guinea pigs.

"What's ... ACHOO! ... going on?" said Violet.

"Mischief looked normal when we saw him the other day. Now he can glow in the dark!" said Poppy.

Everything was falling into place. I'd suspected there wasn't something quite right about the ghostly guinea pigs. Something not quite ghostly enough!

"I don't think the guinea pigs are ghosts!" I said. "Violet is allergic to them, they can eat and poo. They look like normal guinea pigs in the light and one of them is definitely Mischief from the pet store!"

"Whoa!" said Poppy.

"**AChooo!**" sneezed Violet again. "Come on, let's find out. I think it's this way."

7:20 PM
PUDDLEFORD THEATER, BACKSTAGE AGAIN

We picked up the trail of tiny glowing footprints easily. They were still shining in the darkness. Violet couldn't stop sneezing.

The footprints led us to a heavy metal door with a sign that read Props Room. On the floor around it there were more glowing footprints criss-crossing each other in different directions. The door was slightly ajar.

"ACHOO! Achoo!" Violet spluttered. "They must be close; my nose is really itchy!"

"I'll go first," I said, pushing the heavy door open.

creeEEeeeak!

Did the door have to make a ghostly noise? The guinea pigs might not be ghosts, but this was nerve-racking enough. The doorway led down some steps. At the bottom I could see a patch of moonlight coming from a basement window. The room was filled with old theater props. I heard a squeaking noise and the sound of scurrying feet.

"I don't like this," Violet said, as we went down the steps, holding on to each other.

A little ball of glowing fluff whizzed past the bottom of the stairs.

"Stay calm, everyone. The guinea pig we saw on stage was definitely Mischief and he is nothing to be scared of," I said. I tried not to think about how the guinea pigs had attacked each other to get Mrs. Finn's treats.

"ACHOOOOOOOO!" Violet sneezed.

We peeked around the doorway, and for a moment I couldn't believe my eyes. The room was filled with countless glowing ghostly guinea pigs – big ones, small ones, long-haired, and short-haired ones – all running in and out of the props.

Without taking my eyes off the guinea pigs, I felt on the wall for a light switch and clicked it on.

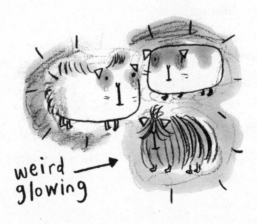

weird →
glowing

161

Now the room was filled with very normal-looking guinea pigs: brown ones, white ones, spotty ones, and blonde ones.

totally normal

A cute little face popped out from behind a stack of jumbled-up old paint cans. I'd have recognized that guinea pig anywhere. I made my way across the room, being careful not to step on any, and picked him up.

"How did you get here, Mischief?" I said. His little whiskers tickled my face.

"Fluffy!" Poppy shouted. She'd spotted the crazy-haired pet store guinea pig. He was sniffing at her ankles.

"Mr. Darcy!" Violet said, scooping up the guinea pig who had given us the slip earlier on.

I looked closely at the cans of paint. They were covered in rust. Hold on – why was there a puddle around them?

"That paint!" I said, realizing what had been going on at last. "It's glow-in-the-dark paint!"

"Poppy, turn the light off again!" I said, dipping my finger in the puddle of paint.

The lights went off and the room filled with the mysterious green glow of the guinea pigs. The puddle of paint was the same ghostly green.

"Whoa! You have a ghostly finger!" Poppy said, staring at my eerily glowing finger.

ghostly finger

One of the guinea pigs ran through the puddle of paint, sending glowing spray everywhere. The green light and the guinea pigs made it look as if there was some sort of weird ghostly disco going on.

"So that's why everyone thought the guinea pigs were ghostly!" Violet said, flicking the light back on.

Poppy started laughing and Violet jumped up and down. But there was still one thing left to explain, and a good Young Super Sleuth ties up all the loose ends. How did Mischief and Fluffy – and all these other guinea pigs – get here from the pet store?

7:25 PM
PUDDLEFORD THEATER PROPS ROOM
(WITH SOME NOT-SO-GHOSTLY GUINEA PIGS)

"Hello? Hello? Are you down there, girls?"
It was Mrs. Finn's panicked voice.

Spangle bounded into the room, his cape
fluttering behind him. The guinea pigs squeaked
and dashed away. Spangle jumped after
them and started pawing and
sniffing at something.

That's when I realized he
was trying to stick his
head into a hole in the
floor. A hole just big
enough for a guinea pig!

Spangle

hole →

"The guinea pigs have burrowed in here!" I said. "I bet I know exactly where this burrow leads to."

Mrs. Finn clomped down the steps in her glittering stiletto boots. "Oh, my goodness! RATS!" she gasped.

"They're not rats," Poppy said, holding Fluffy closer to Mrs. Finn's face. "They're guinea pigs – **your** guinea pigs!"

"My ... what? What on earth is going on?" Mrs. Finn said, clutching the doorframe.

"Mrs. Finn, are you sitting comfortably?" I said, readjusting my fedora hat. "Let me explain what's been going on ..."

(**Wow!** I hardly ever get to say that!)

DETECTIVE CATCHPHRASES: Solving Your Mystery

It's a good idea to sound like a detective at all times. This reassures people that you are professional and excellent at solving mysteries. If you can think of a catchphrase to use when you solve your case, people are more likely to remember who you are and what you do.

Elementary, my dear

....
(insert name of witness/sidekick)

Are you sitting comfortably? Then let me **explain** ...

This mystery is **managed.**

I've **cracked** it like an egg!

All in a **detective** day's work for me!

TOP TIP

Avoid saying things like, "What? You didn't realize what had been going on?" or, "Only a stupid person wouldn't have solved this mystery." This is likely to irritate the person you are solving the mystery for (the client).

5:17 PM
MYSTERY GIRLS HQ

We didn't end up winning the
talent show, although we did
get a runner-up prize.

Mrs. Finn and Spangle won first prize. The
judges said that they did really well to perform
after the chaos with the ghostly guinea pigs.
Apparently some of the other acts refused to
go on stage. They were too scared the ghostly
guinea pigs (who weren't actually ghostly at all)
might attack them.

WARNING

This afternoon, Mrs. Finn invited us to see the new Entertainment and Containment system she built for the guinea pigs. The guinea pigs have got loads of space and toys to occupy them so they don't get into any trouble again.

And – TOTALLY AMAZING! – to say thank you for solving the case, Mrs. Finn has given us Mischief. Mom says we can keep him at Mystery Girls HQ as long as I promise to look after him. The glow-in-the-dark paint hasn't completely washed off so he still has a really ghostly glow at night. He's the perfect mysterious pet!

mischief

So, this is what really happened. Here is my case report in full ...

THE CASE OF THE GHOSTLY GUINEA PIG, SOLVED BY THE MYSTERY GIRLS

The ghostly guinea pigs weren't ghosts at all. They were, in fact, totally normal everyday guinea pigs that had escaped (through an undetected burrow) from Fluff 'n' Feathers pet store. The guinea pigs had managed to dig a burrow from the pet store to the props room in Puddleford theater. This was 50 feet long!

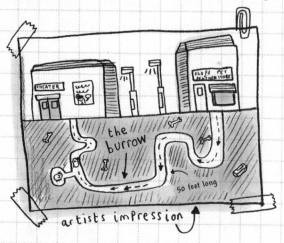

artists impression

The guinea pigs had been covered in glow-in-the-dark paint that had leaked from some old cans being stored in the props room. They'd managed to get themselves totally covered in the stuff.

Mrs. Finn, the pet store owner, had been very busy preparing her act for the talent show (which she won – yay!) and didn't notice that her guinea pigs were up to anything strange.

Also, Mrs. Finn didn't spot the warning signs earlier because her dog, Spangle, had accidentally smashed her glasses during a triple backflip. With the talent show approaching, there was no time to get a new pair.

The pet treats Mrs. Finn bakes are so delicious the guinea pigs kept coming back to the pet store looking for food.

Some guinea pigs managed to escape from the props room by climbing up a stack of glow-in-the-dark paint cans and out through an open basement window (kind of like a cat flap for guinea pigs). This is why we found ghostly poops next to the window.

Eyewitnesses saw ghostly guinea pigs near the theater in the "Triangle of Spookiness." The Mystery Girls have now declared this area to be safe, but if anybody does see a glowing guinea pig on the loose they should try to contain it and return it to Mrs. Finn. There may well be a few guinea pigs still out there. Mrs. Finn is doing her best to round them up using her treats.

The witnesses who encountered the ghostly guinea pigs are all recovering well from the experience. They 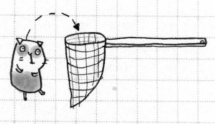 were relieved to discover the guinea pigs were not ghostly after all. (Miss Crumble fell in love with the Mr. Darcy look-a-like guinea pig from the pet store. She decided to get him and call him Mr. Bingley.*)

*Mr. Bingley is also a dashingly handsome character from Miss Crumble's favorite book.

CASE CLOSED

miss Crumble and
Mr. Bingley

ACKNOWLEDGMENTS

Working on these books has been an absolute joy
so I'd just like to say thank you to some important
people who made it all possible:

My lovely partner, Simon Thorpe, for his endless ideas.

My agent, Mark Mills, for having such confidence in
my work, and for spotting an idea.

My editor, Jenny Glencross, for her excellent
facilitation skills, huge enthusiasm and immediate
belief in Mariella.

All at Orion, for spreading the word and helping
Mariella to reach this point.

My amazingly supportive family and friends,
especially Mum and Dad.

A special mention to my brother, Andrew. Without
him as a source of inspiration there would be no
Arthur in this story. (And that wouldn't be half
as funny!)

Kate Pankhurst, 2013